Usborne
Sticker Dolly Dressing
Shopping

Illustrated by Jo Moore

Written by Fiona Watt
Designed by Vicky Arrowsmith

Contents

2   Meet the dolls
4   In a shopping mall
6   Shopping for shoes
8   Christmas shopping
10 Taking a break
12 Paper and pens
13 Browsing for books
14 Toy shopping
16 Beachwear
18 Street market
20 At the sales
22 Party time
24 Shopping for cupcakes
    Stickers

Meet the dolls

Meet Kara, Lauren and Cassie, three schoolfriends who just love to shop. They're waiting for a train that will take them into town for a shopping trip. Kara is hoping to find a new pair of shoes, Lauren's looking for a present for her aunt's new baby and Cassie has been saving for ages for a pretty party dress.

Kara loves going shopping for accessories, such as bangles, belts and bags, that will match her clothes.

In a shopping mall

The dolls are excited as a new shopping mall has just opened nearby. This is their first visit and they've been shopping all morning. Cassie's bought a CD and some pens, Kara has a new bag and a necklace, and Lauren's found a book that she's been longing to read for ages.

Shopping for shoes

Kara has dragged the dolls into the shoe section in a big department store. She's looking for a pair of sandals to match a purple bag that she's just bought. Lauren has spotted some patterned sneakers that she likes and Cassie is trying on some pink pumps.

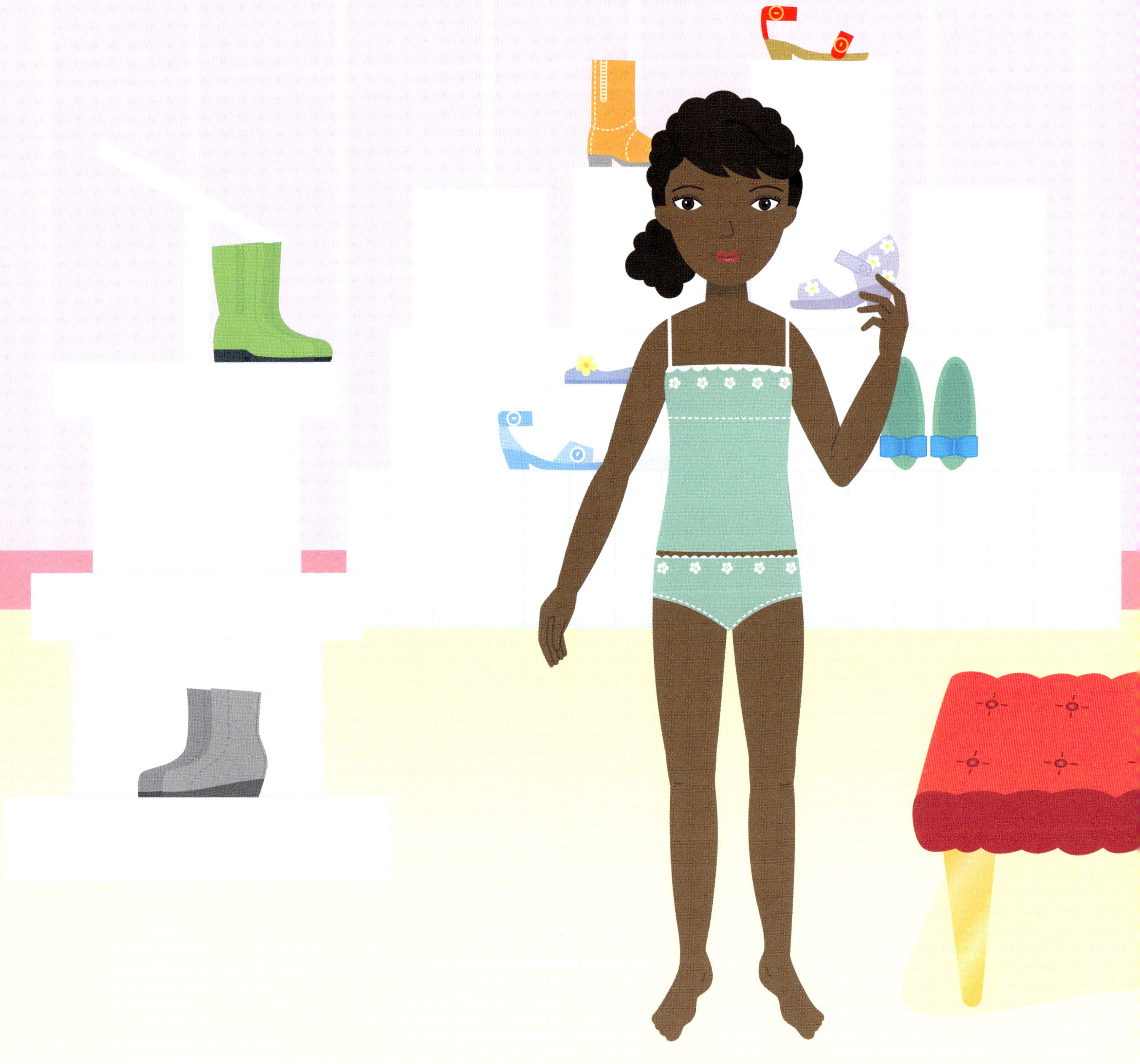

Christmas shopping

Lauren, Cassie and Kara love shopping at Christmas time. They enjoy seeing the decorated window displays and choosing presents for their friends and family. Cassie has bought Lauren a new set of glitter pens, but she's keeping it a surprise!

Taking a break

It's a hot afternoon in summer and the dolls are taking some time out from shopping to have a drink at a pavement café. Kara's chosen a refreshing orange juice, while Cassie has bought a summer-fruit smoothie.

Paper and pens

Lauren loves spending time browsing for new paper, pens and paints for her art projects. She often buys patterned notebooks and folders, and boxes that she can use for storing her art equipment and the things that she makes.

Toy shopping

Lauren's aunt has just had a new baby – a little girl named Lily. Lauren, Kara and Cassie are trying to choose a present for her. Should they get her a fluffy pink bunny with big ears or a mobile that could hang in her bedroom?

Beachwear

Cassie, Kara and Lauren have all outgrown their swimsuits, so they're shopping for new ones. They've each chosen one to try on, and now they are looking at the rest of the department to see if there's anything else they'd like to buy.

Street market

It's Saturday morning and the dolls are shopping in a weekend street market. There are lots of stalls selling handmade clothes and pictures, and lots of accessories and gifts. Lauren has bought a hand-printed T-shirt, while Kara and Cassie have each chosen a new scarf.

At the sales

It's sale time and the dolls are hunting for bargains in a busy department store. Both Lauren and Cassie have spotted T-shirts that they like, and Kara has seen a dress that is half price, that she'd like to try on.

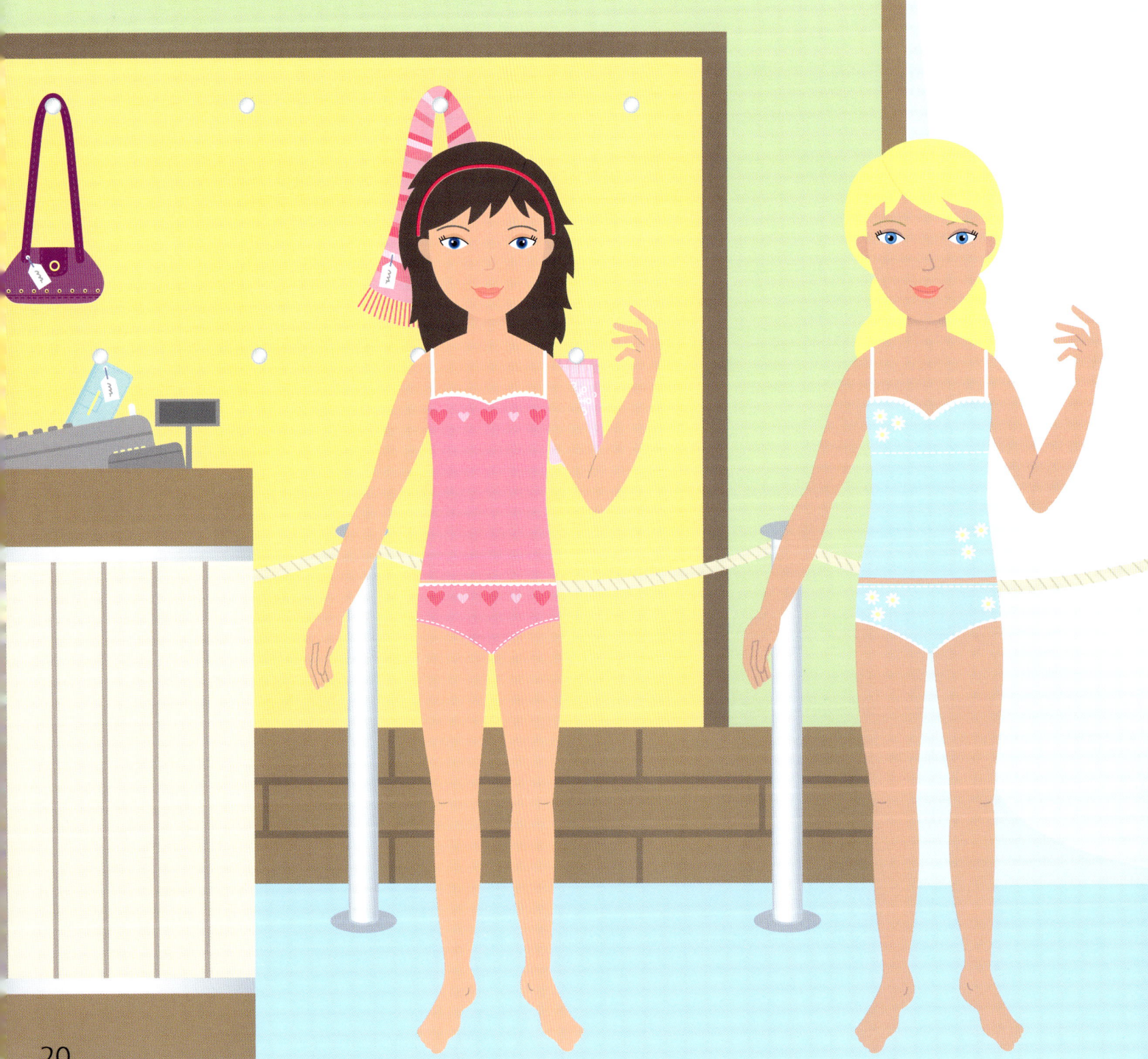

Party time

The dolls have been invited to a summer party and they want to buy new dresses for the occasion. They are trying on the outfits they've picked from the racks and are deciding whether or not to buy them.

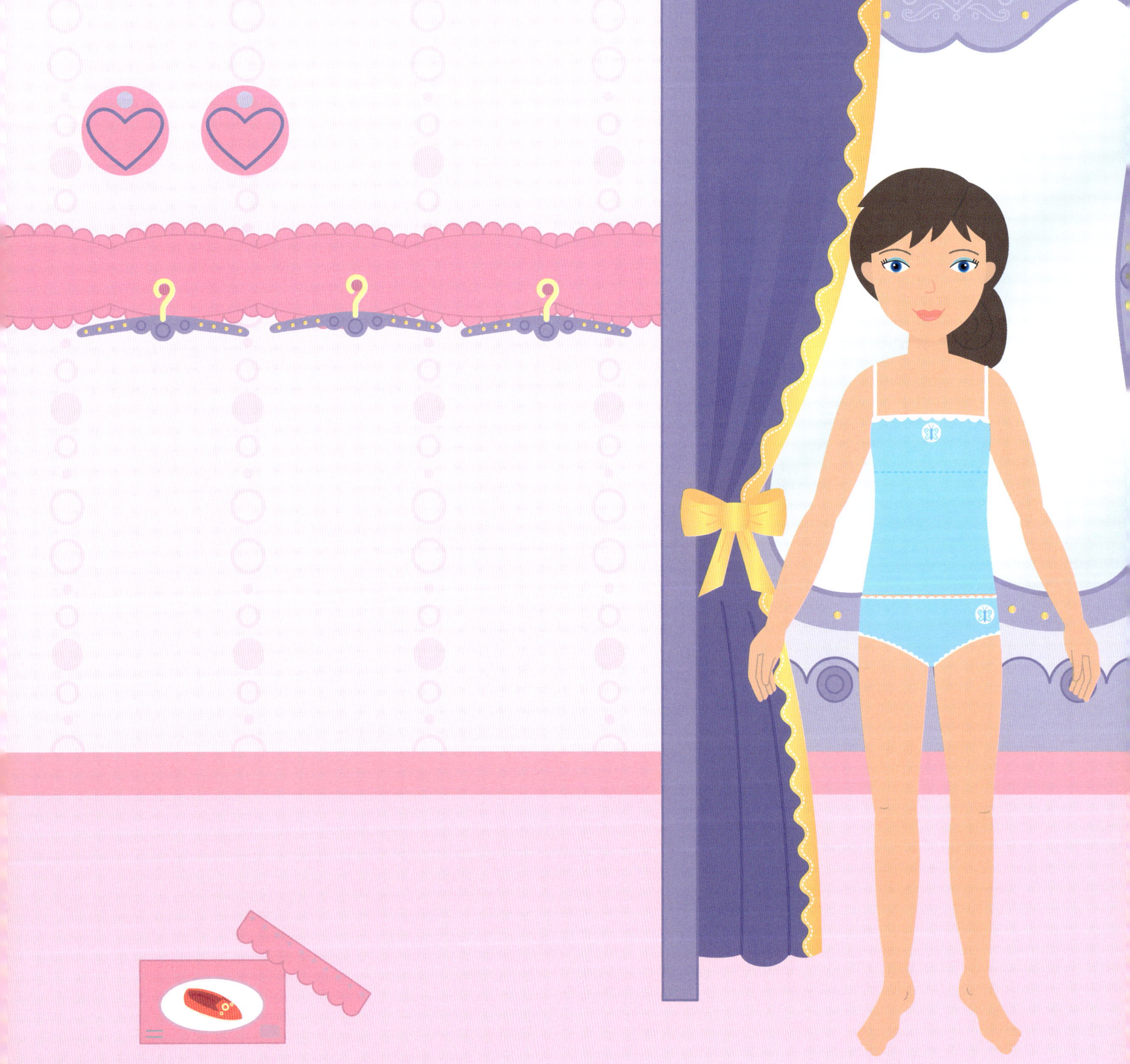

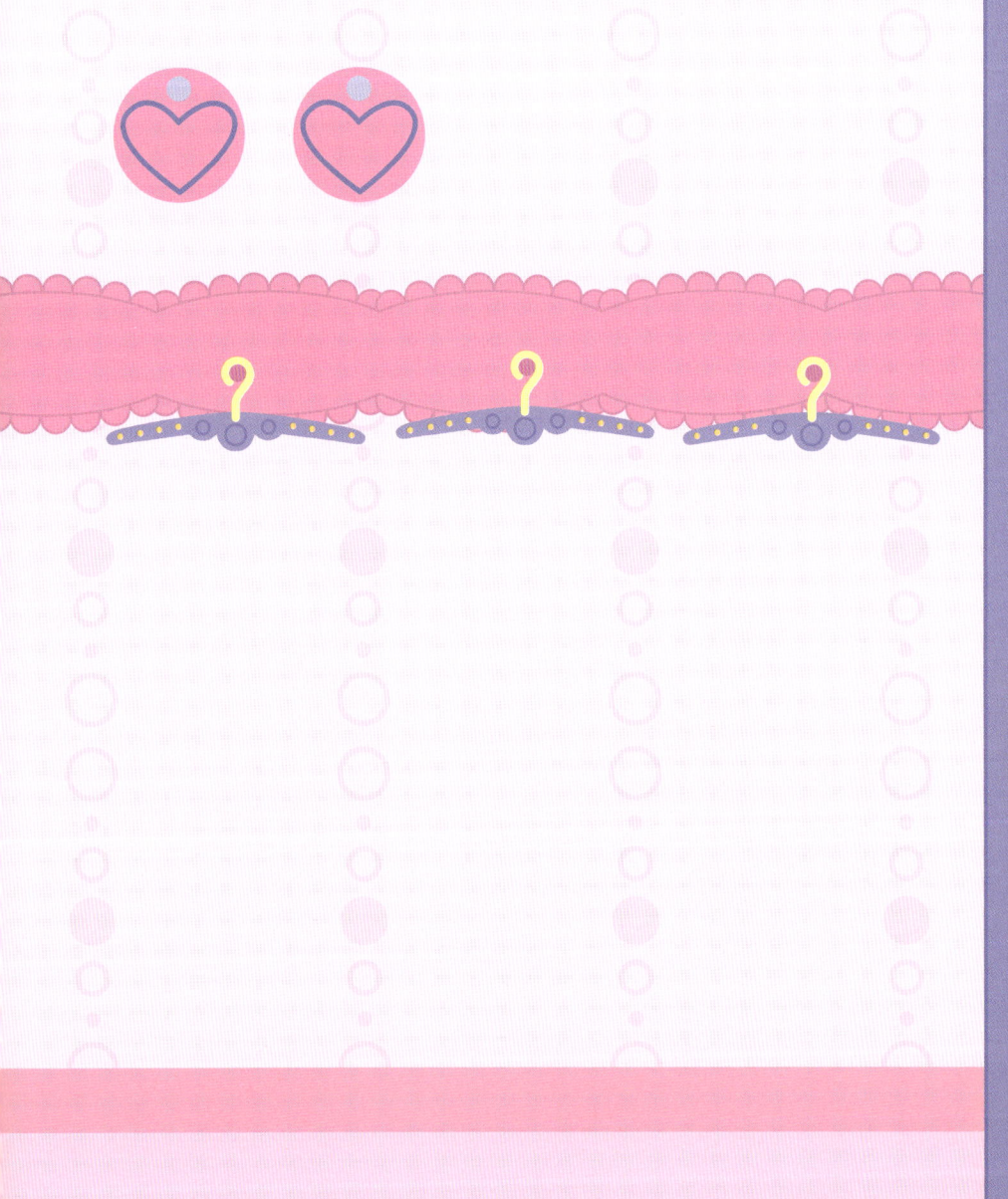

Shopping for cupcakes

The dolls are tired and hungry after a long shopping trip. Cassie has popped into a cake shop to buy something for each of them to eat. She's chosen vanilla, strawberry and chocolate cupcakes for them all to share.

Paper and pens

Page 12

Browsing for books

Page 13

Beachwear

Pages 16-17